Dreams: Visions of the Crow *is an honest exploration of how the journey forward often begins with an understanding of the past. Damon's particular challenges shine an important light on the scars that still need to be healed in many Indigenous communities. This story offers a beautiful message of breaking the cycle of trauma with patience, empathy, and perseverance.*
BRENDA HICKEY, cartoonist, *My Little Pony*, *Butterfly House*

Highly recommend—I read this book in one sitting! In Visions of the Crow, *Wanda John-Kehewin and nicole marie burton have created an immersive world, full of pain and struggle, but also love, friendship, and beauty. And the characters living in that world are complex and compelling—I just had to find out what happened to them.*
SARAH LEAVITT, cartoonist and comics educator

This graphic tale of intersection of the day-to-day, gritty real world and the sometimes intrusive, overwhelming, and hard-to-deal-with vision world is beautifully handled. Fantastic interconnectedness of the various levels of reality explored in the book—consciousness, spirit, family, society, history—with a hopefulness for the future.
IAN PERRY, educator

Always for my children.
—Wanda John-Kehewin

For my mother, Sharon Wenger,
my stepmother, Carla Burton,
and my grandmother, Eleanor Wenger.
—nicole marie burton

Special thanks to
Daisy John of Kehewin Cree Nation,
Master's of Indigenous Languages,
for Plains Cree translation guidance.

VOLUME 1

DREAMS

VISIONS OF THE CROW

Wanda John-Kehewin | nicole marie burton

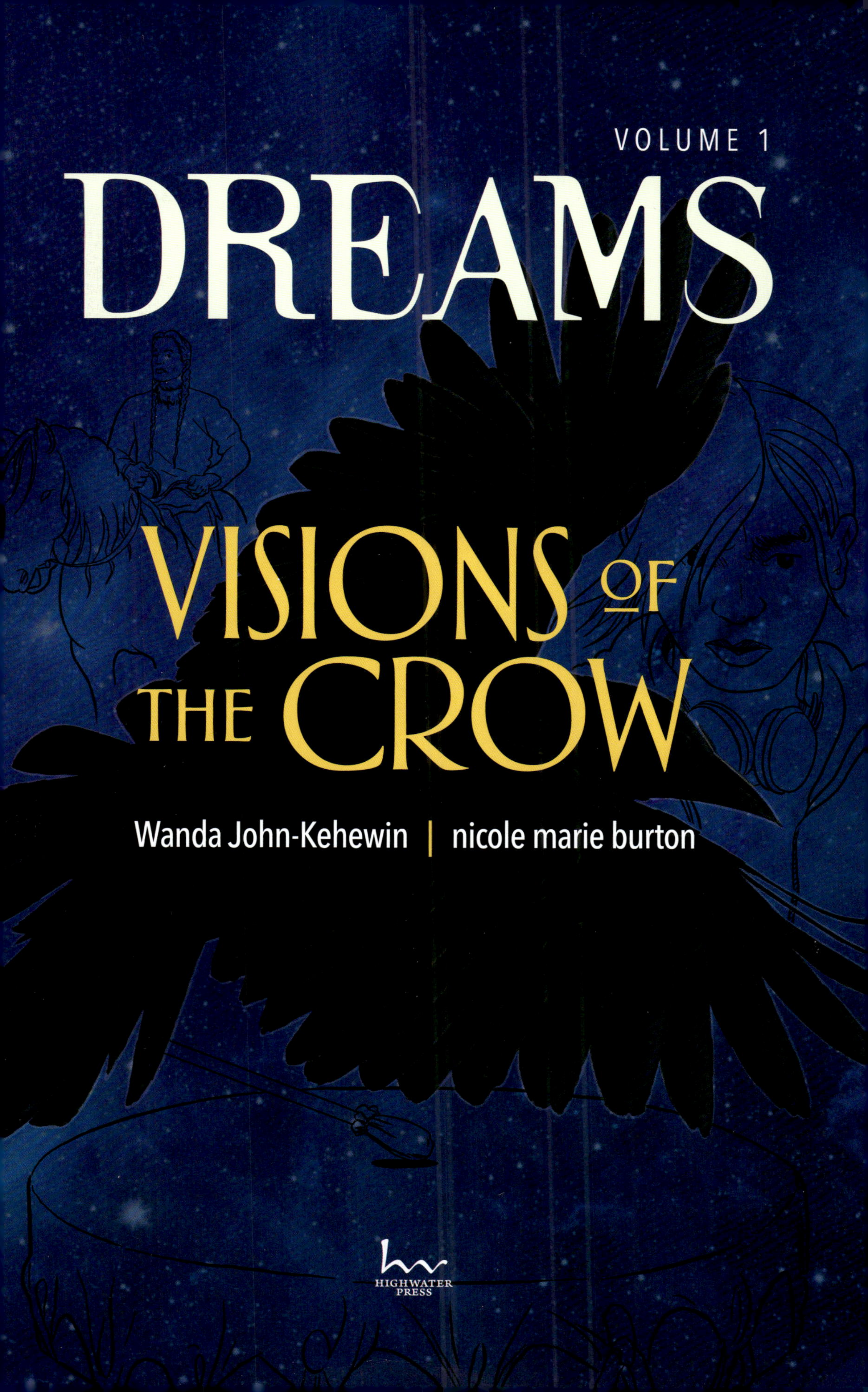

HIGHWATER PRESS

Damon Quinn
ROLLING BUZZSAW
A–M
Stuff NEVER
TWO HANDS GRIPPING THE STEERING WHEEL, LIKE I COULD CONTROL A CAREENING CAR...
PANTS
SOCKS
UNDERW
How to Organize Your Life
How to Organize Your Life

Indigenous Studies Gr. 12
N–Z
"Failure will never overtake me if my determination is strong enough."
Og Mandino
A-Z PUT BACK ALPHABETICALLY OR DIE!!!
LONG SLEEVE
SHORT SLEEVE

DAMON!

DA-A-A-A-M-O-ONNN
YOU GOT ANY MONEY, HON?
NO, I DON'T. I DON'T EVEN HAVE ENOUGH FOR LUNCH.
I DON'T EVEN THINK THERE'S ANYTHING I CAN BRING FOR LUNCH.
GOOD JOB, MARNIE.

PLEASE, DAMON. YOU KNOW WHAT IT'S LIKE WHEN I'M SICK!
PLEASE DON'T START THIS MORNING.
WHEN IS IT EVER A GOOD TIME?
ONEISSIN
TOO BUSY TRYING TO MAKE IT 'TIL TOMORROW. EVERYONE, EVERYBODY, MAKE IT 'TIL TOMORROW. A MANTRA FOR THE DYING.
@#$% THIS! DRINKING ALL THE TIME...ASKING ME FOR MONEY. GOTTA GET OUT OF HERE!

HEY, INDIAN IN THE CUPBOARD! HOW'S YOUR VISION QUEST GOING?
NOTHING BETTER TO DO, MARCUS?
SURE, I COULD KICK THE CRAP OUT OF YOU.
IF THAT'S HOW YOU WANNA SPEND YOUR TIME. WASTING MINE.
OOH...LOOK AT THE INDIAN, SO BRAVE. WATCH OUT! HE MIGHT TURN INTO HIS SPIRIT ANIMAL... A COCKROACH.

GET IT RIGHT, DUMBASS! I'M NOT INDIAN!
YES YOU ARE. I'VE SEEN YOU COME OUT OF THE SUPPORT OFFICE FOR DURKS!
HE ISN'T FULL INDIGENOUS, CAN'T YOU TELL?
STAY OUT OF IT! I DON'T EVEN KNOW YOU!
FWOOSH

perch
ONEISSIN
shoo
GET OFF ME!
HA HA HA HA
HA HA
HA HA
WHOA, DAMON, IS THAT YOUR SPIRIT ANIMAL?
SCREW YOU, MARCUS. IT'S JUST A DUMB OLD CROW.
GRAB

BIG M, LET'S GO. WE HAVE BIGGER FRIES TO FISH.
WTF MAN? FRIES TO FISH?
AND YOU'RE DAMON QUINN, THE MÉTIS CROW WHISPERER, RIGHT?!

PROOF ONE COULD DIE OF SADNESS.
I AIN'T NO HERO.
WOULDN'T KNOW WHO TO SAVE IF I WAS.
TAP-TAP-TAP

MARNIE? MARNIE? I NEED TO ASK YOU SOMETHING.
WHAT? THE HOUSE ON FIRE?
NO, UNFORTUNATELY.
WHAT IS IT THEN?
AM I PART WHITE AND PART INDIAN?
YEAH. YOUR DAD'S MÉTIS. WHERE DO YOU THINK YOU GOT THEM GORGEOUS PEEPERS, A CRACKER JACK BOX? YOUR DAD COULD TRACE HIS ROOTS BACK TO LOUIS RIEL, AND US BACK TO A GREAT CHIEF.
Sigh
AND YOU'RE FIRST NATIONS? FROM WHERE?

WHY DO WE ALWAYS GOTTA BE FROM SOMEWHERE? YEAH I'M INDIAN, FIRST NATIONS, WHATEVER YOU WANNA CALL IT.
FROM WHERE, MARNIE?
CREE, I'M CREE FROM ALBERTA.
DO WE HAVE FAMILY THERE?
THERE'S LOTS OF FAMILY. NOT THAT THEY'D KNOW WHO WE ARE ANYMORE...IT'S BEEN SO LONG.
WHY DON'T WE EVER GO THERE OR SEE THEM?
I LEFT THERE AT 17 WHEN I WAS PREGNANT WITH YOU.
I HAD A BIG FIGHT WITH THEM ABOUT MY DRINKING AND THE GUY I WAS WITH.

DID YOU DRINK WHEN YOU WERE PREGNANT WITH ME?
IN THE BEGINNING, WHEN I DIDN'T KNOW I WAS GONNA HAVE YOU. BUT I STOPPED RIGHT AWAY WHEN I KNEW.
NO WONDER I'M SO WEIRD.
WHY YOU ASKING ALL THESE USELESS QUESTIONS!? WE'RE BETTER OFF WITHOUT THEM! AND YOU'RE NOT WEIRD.
I JUST WANNA KNOW WHERE WE COME FROM!

DAMON QUINN! HOLD UP!
WHERE'S YOUR CROW, DAMON QUINN?
BITE IT, JOURNEY.
INTERESTING HOW YOU KNOW MY NAME.
YEAH, I EVEN LOOKED IT UP. IT MEANS TO GO SOMEWHERE. NOW GET LOST!
LOOK MAN, I'M NEW HERE AND YOU SEEM KINDA COOL, WITH THE CROW AND ALL.
THAT'S NOT MY STUPID CROW.
COME ON, US INDIANS GOTTA STICK TOGETHER.
US INDIANS? WTF. YOU DON'T ACT ANYTHING LIKE AN INDIAN.
YOU ARE ONE ANGRY JERK. GUESS YOU'D RATHER BE ALONE WITH YOUR BIRDBRAIN BUDDY!

TODAY WE'RE GOING TO DISCUSS CANADA'S HISTORY WITH INDIGENOUS PEOPLES.
HEY, DAMON...WE ALREADY KNOW HOW MUCH SPACE YOU INDIANS TAKE UP. IT'S THE LAMEST STORY EVER TOLD.
DAMON, GO TO THE PRINCIPAL'S OFFICE. **NOW!**

THAT'S A SURE-FIRE WAY TO GET KICKED OUTTA SCHOOL FOR GOOD.
LEAVE ME ALONE. I DON'T CARE ABOUT BEING KICKED OUT.
I'M ONLY TRYING TO HELP.
I DON'T NEED YOUR HELP. I HEARD YOU'RE THE ONE WHO NEEDS HELP. NOW STOP BOTHERING ME!
YOU'RE NOT THE ONLY ONE WITH PROBLEMS, YOU KNOW!

WHY DO YOU KEEP FOLLOWING ME? WHY DO YOU CARE?
BECAUSE WE NEED TO STICK TOGETHER. WHO ELSE IS GOING TO CARE?
LOOK, THERE'S YOUR CROW.
IF IT WAS MY CROW, I'D TRAIN IT TO PECK ALL THEIR EYEBALLS OUT.
SOUNDS LIKE WE WATCH THE SAME KINDA MOVIES.

YOU CAUGHT ME OFF GUARD WHEN YOU ASKED ABOUT FAMILY.
THAT'S 'BOUT THE ONLY THING THAT CAN...I HAVEN'T SPOKEN TO THEM IN YEARS.
COME SIT NEXT TO ME, DAMON.
I LEFT THE RESERVE WHEN I WAS 17. I COULDN'T STAND THE DYSFUNCTION ALL AROUND ME.
YOU HAD TO GO A WHOLE PROVINCE AWAY?
I WAS PREGNANT WITH YOU. ME AND YOUR DAD CAME TO VANCOUVER. THOUGHT WE COULD RUN FROM OUR PASTS AND START FRESH.
I DON'T THINK YOUR DAD COULD HANDLE BEING A DAD. HE CAME FROM THE SAME PLACE I DID.
THE LAST TIME I SAW HIM WAS WHEN YOU WERE FOUR.
WHAT KIND OF GUY WAS HE?

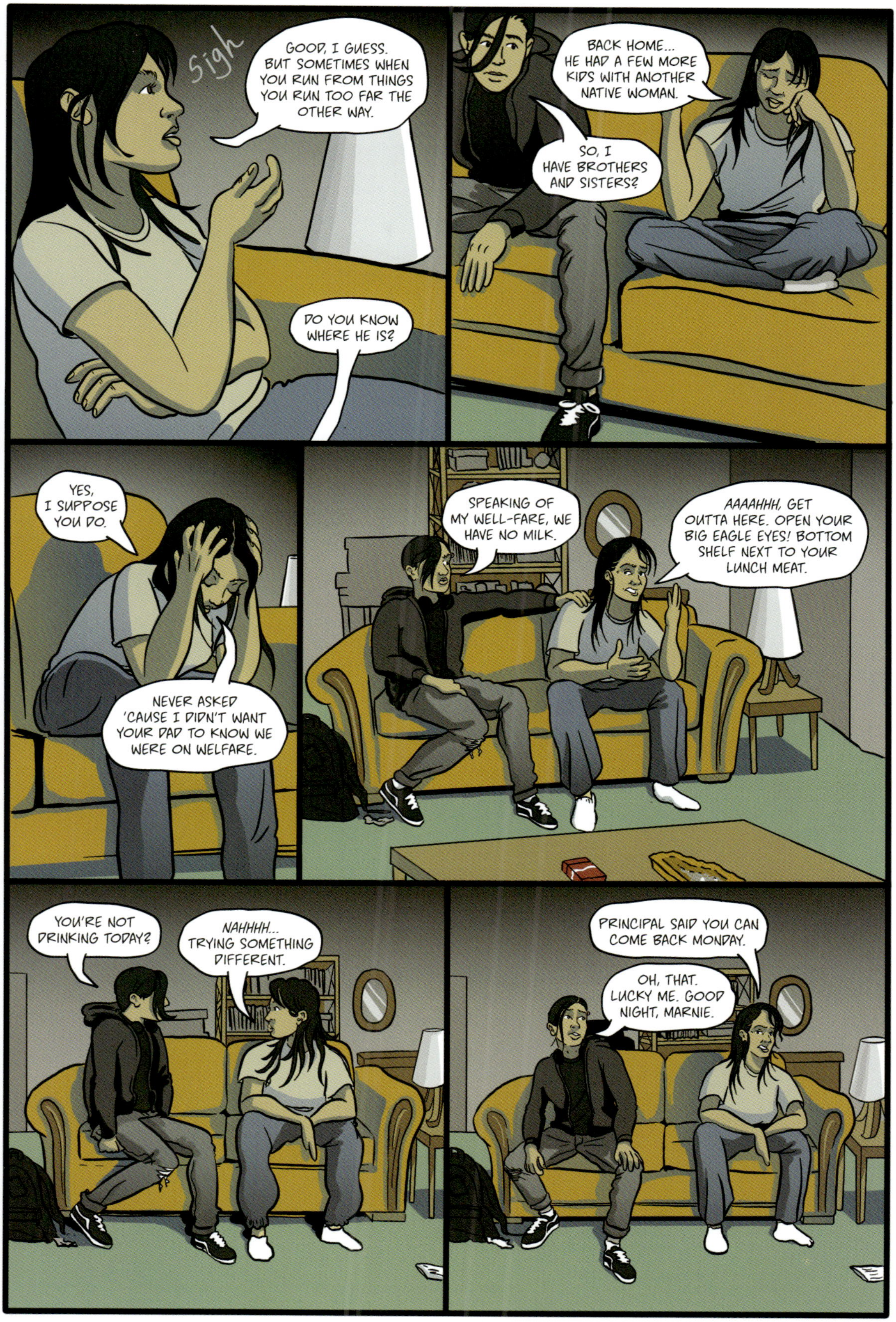
Sigh
GOOD, I GUESS. BUT SOMETIMES WHEN YOU RUN FROM THINGS YOU RUN TOO FAR THE OTHER WAY.
DO YOU KNOW WHERE HE IS?
BACK HOME... HE HAD A FEW MORE KIDS WITH ANOTHER NATIVE WOMAN.
SO, I HAVE BROTHERS AND SISTERS?
YES, I SUPPOSE YOU DO.
NEVER ASKED 'CAUSE I DIDN'T WANT YOUR DAD TO KNOW WE WERE ON WELFARE.
SPEAKING OF MY WELL-FARE, WE HAVE NO MILK.
AAAAHHH, GET OUTTA HERE. OPEN YOUR BIG EAGLE EYES! BOTTOM SHELF NEXT TO YOUR LUNCH MEAT.
YOU'RE NOT DRINKING TODAY?
NAHHHH... TRYING SOMETHING DIFFERENT.
PRINCIPAL SAID YOU CAN COME BACK MONDAY.
OH, THAT. LUCKY ME. GOOD NIGHT, MARNIE.

ONEISSIN
I'VE BEEN WAITING FOR YOU.
ME? &%$#!
ANGRY MUCH?
WHAT KIND OF ELDER TALKS LIKE THAT?
THE KIND OF ELDER THAT THINKS YOU SWEAR TOO MUCH. YOU SHOULD LEARN TO SWEAR IN YOUR OWN LANGUAGE PERHAPS.
HA HA HA

WHY AM I DREAMING OF INDIAN PEOPLE?
BECAUSE YOU'RE INDIGENOUS? YOU'RE ONLY INDIAN IF YOU COME FROM INDIA. DO YOU COME FROM INDIA?
UMM, I DON'T SMOKE.
WELL, DAMON QUINN, IT'S JUST A DREAM. TAKE THE PIPE.
COUGH
COUGH
THOUGHT YOU SAID THIS WAS A DREAM?
YEAH...MINE.
HAHAHA

DO YOU KNOW WHY YOU ARE "DREAMING" ABOUT THIS?
NOT A FRIGGIN' CLUE.
YOUR ANCESTORS HAVE CALLED US TO HELP YOU.
I THINK Y'ALL HAVE THE WRONG NUMBER.
THIS PIPE IS SIX GENERATIONS OLD. ASK KI-KÂWIY ABOUT IT.
MARNIE?
YOUR MOTHER. TO YOU, SHE'S NI-KÂWIY.

COUGH
COUGH
04:00 AM PM
ARE YOU OK?
I'M FINE, MOM. JUST A WEIRD DREAM.
WHY DOES IT SMELL LIKE SMOKE IN HERE?
I SMOKED IN MY DREAMS, NI-KÂWIY.
NI-KÂWIY?
WHAT DID YOU SAY? NI-KÂWIY? DAMON! I USED TO CALL MY MOM THAT. DAMON!
ZZZ

MORNING.
HOW'D YOU GET IN HERE?
THE CROW LET ME IN.
WANT SOME?
HAPPY-O's
NAH, ALL THAT CRAP IS BAD FOR THE GUTS.
HA! I'LL BET YOUR MAKEUP HAS THE SAME INGREDIENTS AS MY CEREAL!
OWW!
WHO'S YOUR FRIEND, DAMON?
MARNIE, MEET JOURNEY. JOURNEY, THIS IS THE ONE AND ONLY MARNIE.

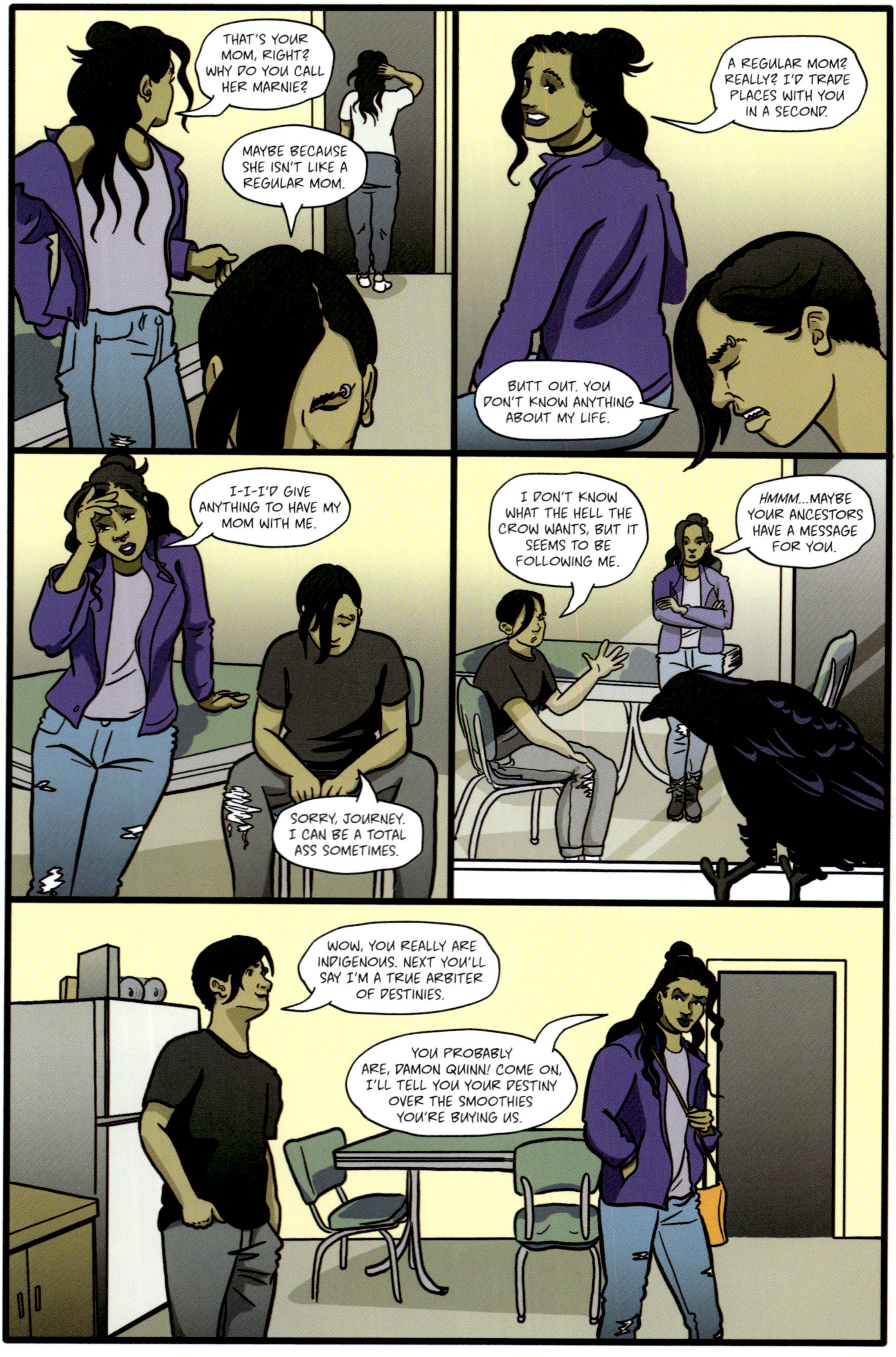
THAT'S YOUR MOM, RIGHT? WHY DO YOU CALL HER MARNIE?
MAYBE BECAUSE SHE ISN'T LIKE A REGULAR MOM.
A REGULAR MOM? REALLY? I'D TRADE PLACES WITH YOU IN A SECOND.
BUTT OUT. YOU DON'T KNOW ANYTHING ABOUT MY LIFE.
I-I-I'D GIVE ANYTHING TO HAVE MY MOM WITH ME.
SORRY, JOURNEY. I CAN BE A TOTAL ASS SOMETIMES.
I DON'T KNOW WHAT THE HELL THE CROW WANTS, BUT IT SEEMS TO BE FOLLOWING ME.
HMMM...MAYBE YOUR ANCESTORS HAVE A MESSAGE FOR YOU.
WOW, YOU REALLY ARE INDIGENOUS. NEXT YOU'LL SAY I'M A TRUE ARBITER OF DESTINIES.
YOU PROBABLY ARE, DAMON QUINN! COME ON, I'LL TELL YOU YOUR DESTINY OVER THE SMOOTHIES YOU'RE BUYING US.

WOW! THIS IS SUPER COOL. DO YOU KNOW MUCH ABOUT NATIVE CULTURES?
NOPE. YOU AND ME, WE LOST A LOT OF OUR PEOPLES BECAUSE OF COLONIZATION. THAT'S THE REAL INDIGENOUS HISTORY.
MY GIGI SAYS I HAVE A LIFETIME OF LEARNING. GIGI MEANS GRANDMOTHER IN THE NISGA'A LANGUAGE.
LEARNING ABOUT WHERE WE CAME FROM TELLS US WHERE WE NEED TO GO.
HEY, YOU'RE LIKE A WISE OLD LADY IN A YOUNG PERSON'S BODY.
IT'S YOU! THE ONE FROM MY DREAMS! YOU WERE SMOKING THE PIPE!
WHAT!? YOU'RE SMOKING THE PIPE! THE WRONG KINDA PIPE!

UNION GOSPEL MISSION
UNION GOSPEL STATION
WHOA! THAT WAS WEIRD.
YEAH, REALLY WEIRD.
CAW!
STUMBLE

THEY WANT US TO SIGN WHITE PAPERS CALLED TREATY 6.
TÂPWÊ! DON'T SIGN!
SIGN THEIR WHITE PAPERS, MISTAHI MASKWA!
WHAT DO YOU THINK, DAMON QUINN?
NOTHING TO SAY? LOOK AT WHAT'S GOING ON AROUND YOU--UNLESS YOU'RE TOO BUSY FEELING SORRY FOR YOURSELF.
WHATEVER YOU SAY, OLD MAN.
WE KNOW EACH AND EVERY ONE OF YOU. YOU ALL HAVE THOUSANDS OF ANCESTORS BEHIND YOU. WHY ARE YOU ALL SO SCARED?

SCARED? OF TREATY 6?
IF WE SIGN THE TREATY, WE LOSE ALL THE LAND. IF WE DON'T SIGN, WE STARVE.
IF WE DON'T SIGN, WE'LL BE HUNGRY! ALL THE BUFFALO ARE GONE! OUR PEOPLE ARE FADING AWAY!
WE CAN'T SIGN! YOU HEARD OKIMÂW. WE SHOULD HOLD OUT FOR BETTER TERMS!
YOU'RE NOT THINKING OF OUR WOMEN AND CHILDREN!
YOU'RE BEING A PRAIRIE CHICKEN! STAY STRONG AND WE'LL GET BETTER TERMS.
Grrrr
grunt
FIGHTING LIKE THIS WON'T SOLVE YOUR PROBLEMS. THEY WANT YOU TO BE DIVIDED!

HONK!
I'M CALLING THE COPS!
HONK!
HONK!
GET OFF THE ROAD, STUPID KID!
ARE YOU OKAY? YOU WENT COMPLETELY NUTS AND RAN ALL OVER THE ROAD!
IT WAS LIKE MY DREAM...ABOUT AN ELDER, ONLY THIS TIME I WAS AWAKE!
AM I GOING CRAZY, JOURNEY?
COME ON, THE COPS ARE ON THEIR WAY!

click
DAMON?! COME HERE!
OLD MAN SAL CALLED AND SAID YOU WERE FREAKING OUT IN THE MIDDLE OF THE ROAD. I DON'T LIKE YOU HANGING OUT WITH THAT GIRL.
DAMON, WHAT'S GOING ON? FIRST YOU'RE SUSPENDED AND NOW YOU'RE PULLING...DANGEROUS STUNTS.
IT'S HARD TO EXPLAIN, MOM.
TRY ME. I'VE HEARD SOME REAL DOOZIES IN THE PAST.
I'VE BEEN HAVING THESE INTENSE DREAMS OR SOMETHING, MORE LIKE NIGHTMARES.
I HAD ONE THE OTHER NIGHT BUT THAT WAS OKAY BECAUSE I WAS IN BED. THIS TIME I WAS IN THE MIDDLE OF THE BUSY STREET AND IF JOURNEY HADN'T BEEN THERE...
I THINK YOU NEED TO TALK TO SOMEONE. NO ONE HAS DREAMS WHEN THEY'RE AWAKE, DAMON.

ONEISSIN
Craig Ben Bolton
411 Cedar Road
HELLO, DAMON QUINN. I'M CRAIG BEN BOLTON. GOOD TO MEET YOU FACE-TO-FACE.
YOU CAN SIT OR LIE DOWN IF YOU'D LIKE.
SOOO...YOUR MOM IS HELLA WORRIED ABOUT YOU.
WHAT!? YEAH ...I GUESS.
WELL, ARE YOU WORRIED ABOUT YOU?
SORTA.

MAN OF MANY WORDS, AREN'T YOU? I CAN'T KEEP UP.
THAT'S THE THING, I DON'T GET IT. I'VE BEEN HAVING THESE STRANGE DREAMS...THEY HAPPEN EVEN WHEN I'M AWAKE.
UH-HUH.
AND...WELL...THERE'S THIS STUPID CROW FOLLOWING ME AROUND.
YOU MEAN THAT CROW AT THE WINDOW?
THAT'S HIM! THAT'S THE CROW.
MAYBE THE CROW HAS ALWAYS FOLLOWED YOU.

ALWAYS FOLLOWED ME? NOW WHO'S THE CRAZY ONE?
MAYBE I DON'T EVEN SEE A CROW...
NAH, JUST PULLING YOUR LEG.
HA HA HA
NUTS. OUR TIME'S UP. SEE YOU NEXT SATURDAY.
AND GO EASY ON KI-KÂWIY, OKAY?
HOW DID HE KNOW THE WORD 'KI-KÂWIY'? HE MUST BE CREE.

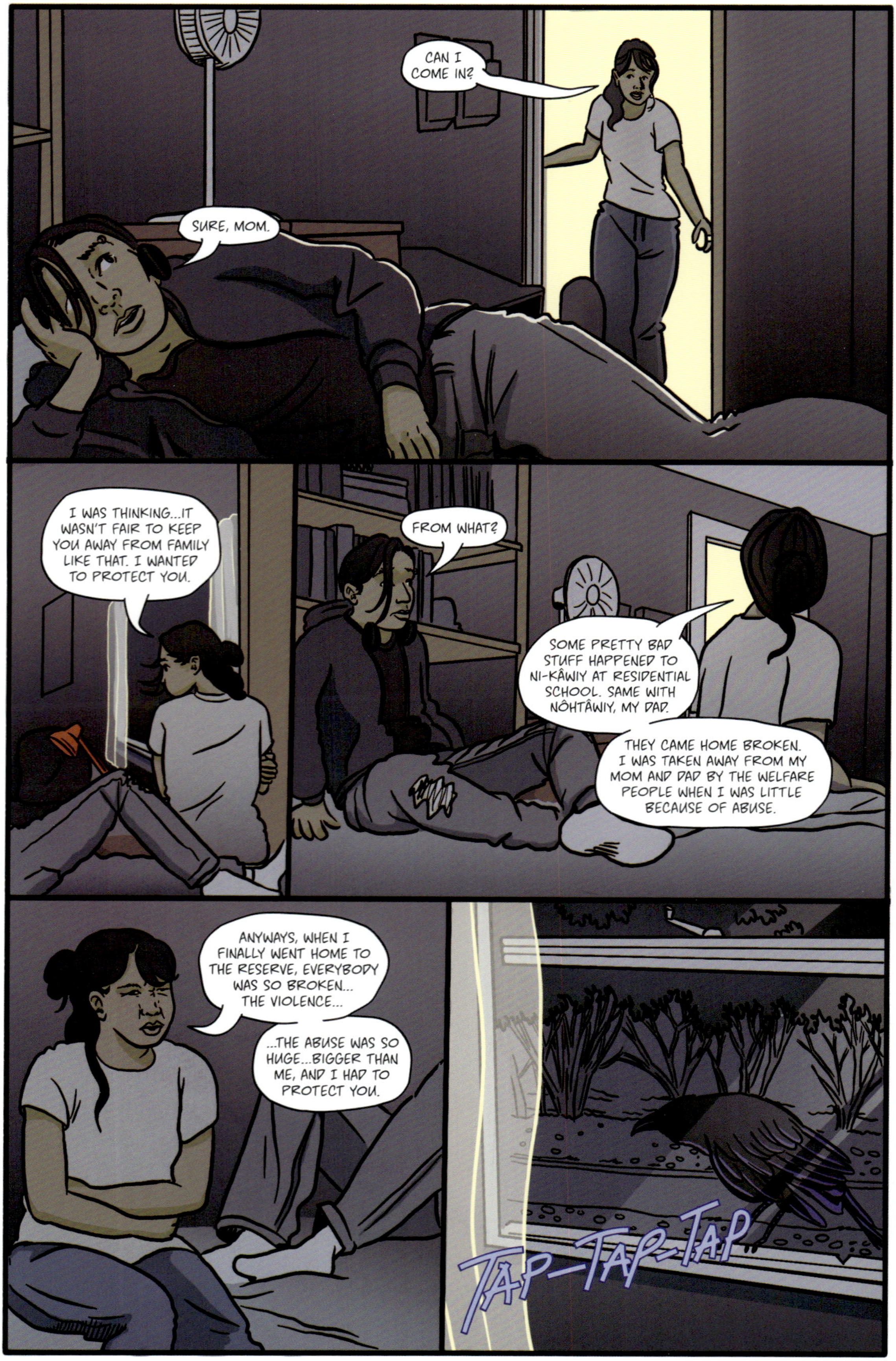
CAN I COME IN?
SURE, MOM.
I WAS THINKING...IT WASN'T FAIR TO KEEP YOU AWAY FROM FAMILY LIKE THAT. I WANTED TO PROTECT YOU.
FROM WHAT?
SOME PRETTY BAD STUFF HAPPENED TO NI-KÂWIY AT RESIDENTIAL SCHOOL. SAME WITH NÔHTÂWIY, MY DAD.
THEY CAME HOME BROKEN. I WAS TAKEN AWAY FROM MY MOM AND DAD BY THE WELFARE PEOPLE WHEN I WAS LITTLE BECAUSE OF ABUSE.
ANYWAYS, WHEN I FINALLY WENT HOME TO THE RESERVE, EVERYBODY WAS SO BROKEN... THE VIOLENCE...
...THE ABUSE WAS SO HUGE...BIGGER THAN ME, AND I HAD TO PROTECT YOU.
TAP-TAP-TAP

THAT DAMN CROW HAS BEEN FOLLOWING ME EVERYWHERE!
HE'S ACTUALLY KNOCKING ON THE WINDOW.
NOHKOM USED TO SAY CROWS ARE VERY WISE AND CAN CARRY MESSAGES. WHAT WOULD HAPPEN IF WE OPENED THE WINDOW?
SWOOSH
WHAT IS IT?
HELL IF I KNOW. IT LOOKS LIKE A HUGE DOG NAIL!
THIS ISN'T A DOG'S NAIL, IT'S A BEAR CLAW!
WHAT KIND OF GIFT IS THAT?
A CROW DROPPED A BEAR CLAW IN THE MIDDLE OF YOUR BED! IT'S A GIFT!
THE CREE HAVE A STRONG RESPECT FOR MASKWA, THE BEAR. THIS HERE IS A BLACK BEAR CLAW.
I'VE ONLY SEEN A CLAW LIKE THIS ONE OTHER TIME. NI-TÂNISKOTÂPÂN, GREAT-GREAT-GRANDFATHER, HAD A MASKWA TÂPISKÂKAN, BEAR NECKLACE. THIS IS SPECIAL, DAMON.

BUS STOP #
WELL LOOK WHO IT IS...OUR FAVOURITE INDIAN IN THE CUPBOARD OUT IN THE WORLD.
CAN I HELP YOU, BRO?
YEAH, YOU CAN HELP ME TO MESS YOU UP.
CAW!
CAW!
CAW!
HA HA HA HA
%$#@!!! THIS IS ON YOU, DAMON!
ME? HA! IF I COULD GET CROWS TO MESS YOU UP, THAT'D BE AWESOME!
CAW!

BUS STOP #

OH NI-KIHCI-ÂNISKOTÂPÂN!
UH...HELLO.
MY NAME IS ISABELLE.
I AM KI-KIHCI-ÂNISKOTÂPÂN, YOUR GREAT-GREAT-GREAT-GRANDMOTHER. I AM SO HAPPY TO SEE YOU!
REALLY? YOU DON'T LOOK THAT OLD!
NOBODY'S OLD IN THE SPIRIT REALM!
I WANT TO INTRODUCE YOU TO NIMOSÔM, MY GRAND-UNCLE, WHO IS A SINGER.
KIHIW, THIS IS DAMON QUINN, YOUR OTANSKOTAPAN, GREAT-NEPHEW! ISN'T HE HANDSOME?
HELLO THERE, NEPHEW. YOU HERE TO SING?
NOT REALLY, I DON'T SING.
EVERYBODY SINGS. SOME DON'T SOUND SO GOOD, BUT THAT DOESN'T STOP THEM. WE SING TO OUR SPIRIT AND TO KISEMANITO.
STILL NOT SINGING, NOT EVEN IN THE SHOWER. NOT EVEN IN A DREAM.
AWWW...HAS THE CRAZY WORLD BEEN TOO HARD ON YOU? FORGET WHAT OTHERS THINK.

NEPHEW, OUR VOICE WAS GIVEN TO US BY KISEMANITO AND WE SHOULD NOT BE AFRAID TO SPEAK UP. THAT INCLUDES SINGING. BESIDES, NO ONE CAN HEAR YOU IN A DREAM.
FIRST RULE IS TO ALWAYS RESPECT THE DRUM. A DEER GAVE ITS LIFE TO FEED US AND MAKE THIS DRUM, SO WE MUST NEVER LAY IT ON ITS FACE.
THIS DRUM WILL BE YOURS ONE DAY. YOU DON'T HAVE TO SEARCH FOR IT. IT WILL FIND YOU.
FOLLOW MY BEAT. NOT TOO HARD AND NOT TOO SOFT. JUST ENOUGH THAT IT FEELS RIGHT IN YOUR SPIRIT AND IN YOUR BODY.
TÂPWÊ, LIKE THAT, NEPHEW. NOW LISTEN WHEN I SING AND COPY ME. JUST DO YOUR BEST.
THUM
THUM
THUM

THUM THUM THUM
EVERYONE THINKS THEY'RE A ROCK STAR.

CHATTY AS USUAL. WHY DON'T YOU CLOSE YOUR EYES FOR A FEW MINUTES?
TAKE A DEEP BREATH...IN...OUT... IN...OUT.

HOW? WHAT?! WHAT ARE WE DOING HERE?
YOU TELL ME, DAMON QUINN. IT'S YOUR VISION.
ONEISSIN
WANT TO TALK ABOUT IT? YOUR MUSICAL BUS TRIP... THE VISIONS?
HOW DO YOU KNOW ABOUT THE BUS?
DAMON QUINN, TIME TO FESS UP--NOTHING TO LOSE IN A DREAM.
MORE LIKE A NIGHTMARE, WITH ME SINGING MY LUNGS OUT ON THE BUS. SO UNCOOL.
THERE'S THAT CROW AGAIN!
MAYBE THAT CROW IS A MESSENGER, WINGING IT ALONG WITH YOU ON YOUR JOURNEY.

I'M TOTALLY LOST.
YOU WERE LOST, DAMON QUINN, BUT YOUR SPIRIT CALLED OUT TO THE ANCESTORS IN YOUR TIME OF NEED.
SOMETIMES THEY TAKE A FEW BUSINESS YEARS TO GET BACK TO YOU.
YOU'RE NEARLY A MAN, DAMON QUINN.
IT'S TIME TO CARRY THE ANCESTORS' WISHES FORWARD.
I-I-I HAVE DARK THOUGHTS...LIKE, SOMETIMES I JUST WANT TO SLEEP AND MAYBE NOT WAKE UP. MY LIFE ISN'T GOING SO WELL.
MY MOM DRINKS ALL THE TIME. I GO HUNGRY SOMETIMES. PEOPLE AT SCHOOL PUSH ME AROUND. I HAVE NO FRIENDS...
YOU HAVE ALL THE FRIENDS YOU NEED. LOOK AT THE CROW HELPING YOU MAKE YOUR LONG JOURNEY.
THESE ARE MISÂSKWATÔMINA, SASKATOONS. ONE OF OUR MAINSTAYS AS CREE PEOPLE. THEY ALSO FIX A CASE OF THE STUCKS!

I DIDN'T KNOW BERRIES COULD TASTE SO GOOD...AND IN A DREAM TO BOOT! THE STUCKS?
LIKE I SAID, DAMON QUINN, DON'T EAT TOO MANY OR YOU'LL HAVE A SEVERE CASE OF THE RUNS.
I CAN EAT AS MANY AS I WANT 'CAUSE IT'S A DREAM! MMMM...THESE ARE GOOD!
THIS MAY BE A LONG WALK, EVEN IN A DREAM.
WHY ARE YOU DOING THAT IF THIS IS A DREAM?
HEY, WHERE'D YOU GO?
Z-Z-Z-Z
HE'S BUSHED FROM A DREAM WALK?

HAVE YOU EVER HAD MISÂSKWATÔMINA?
IN THE REA HUNGRY G
OF COURSE. IS THAT WHY YOUR LIPS ARE PURPLE, LIKE YOU'VE BEEN PUNCHED IN THE MOUTH?
WHERE DID YOU HAVE MISÂSKWATÔMINA? I HAVEN'T HAD THOSE IN AGES! I WOULD LOVE SOME.
WAIT, I MIGHT STILL HAVE SOME!
DON'T EAT TOO MANY, YOU'LL GET THE RUNS.
WORTH IT! I HAVEN'T EATEN MISÂSKWATÔMINA IN SUCH A LONG TIME!
MOM? DO YOU KNOW ANYTHING ABOUT THE SPIRIT?
DID YOUR COUNSELLOR TELL YOU ABOUT THAT?

NI-KÂWIY USED TO TALK ABOUT THAT A LOT.
IN THE REALM OF HUNGRY GHOSTS GABOR MATÉ
SHE'D SAY DRINKING HURT YOUR SPIRIT, BUT SHE'D DO IT ANYWAY. I GET IT, THOUGH. REALLY EASY TO RUN FROM PAIN. SOME PEOPLE MANAGE TO QUIT...
HEY, DO YOU THINK WE COULD GO VISIT FAMILY IN ALBERTA?
Y--YOU KNOW, IF THEY ARE UP FOR A VISIT?
MAYBE IT'S SOMETHING WE CAN DO, BUT YOU'D HAVE TO WORK A BIT SO WE COULD SAVE ENOUGH TO GO.
I BET I COULD FIND A JOB.

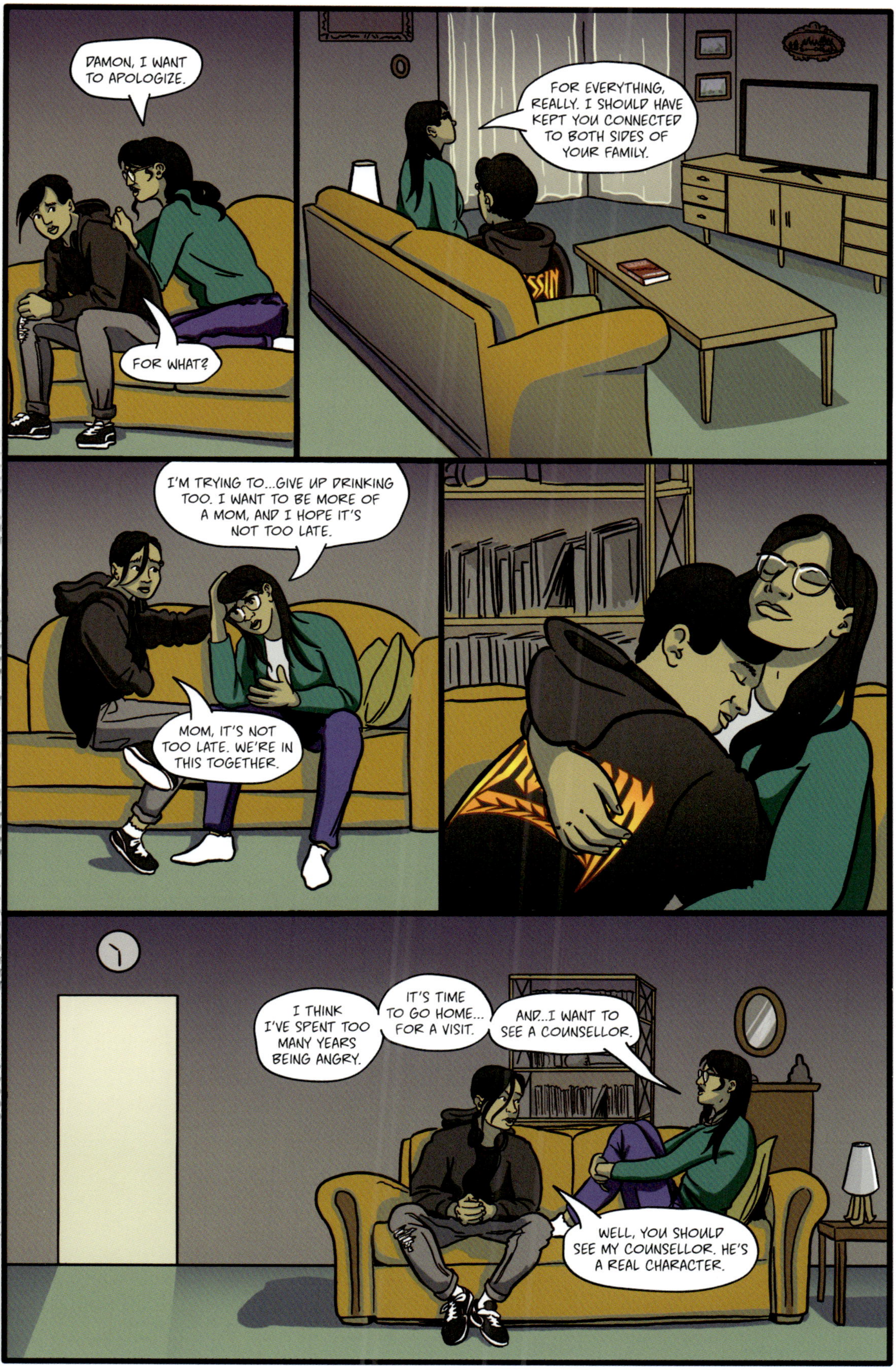
DAMON, I WANT TO APOLOGIZE.
FOR WHAT?
FOR EVERYTHING, REALLY. I SHOULD HAVE KEPT YOU CONNECTED TO BOTH SIDES OF YOUR FAMILY.
I'M TRYING TO...GIVE UP DRINKING TOO. I WANT TO BE MORE OF A MOM, AND I HOPE IT'S NOT TOO LATE.
MOM, IT'S NOT TOO LATE. WE'RE IN THIS TOGETHER.
I THINK I'VE SPENT TOO MANY YEARS BEING ANGRY.
IT'S TIME TO GO HOME... FOR A VISIT.
AND...I WANT TO SEE A COUNSELLOR.
WELL, YOU SHOULD SEE MY COUNSELLOR. HE'S A REAL CHARACTER.

Journey
JOURNEY?
HEY, DAMON QUINN! WHERE YOU BEEN? TO LONDON TO SEE THE KING?
THE KING? MORE LIKE A ROYAL PAIN IN THE ASS!
THAT DOESN'T EVEN MAKE SENSE, DAMON QUINN.
150 Years Retold
THIS PLACE

EVER SINCE I MET YOU, NOTHING MAKES SENSE!
FAMOUS LAST WORDS. SO, HAVE YOU HAD ANY MORE EPISODES?
LOOK, HOW 'BOUT WE MEET UP TOMORROW? I'LL SPRING FOR LUNCH 'CAUSE I NEED TO FIND A JOB.
THAT DOESN'T MAKE SENSE EITHER, BUT YEAH, YOU DO NEED TO FIND A JOB.
MEET ME AT THE BUS STOP ON 12TH AT NOON.
FAMOUS LAST WORDS.
TOMORROW, DAMON QUINN.

THAT YOU, JOURNEY?
YUP, IT'S ME, THE ONE AND ONLY.
WOW, JOURNEY. YOU LOOK WEIRD...DIFFERENT...
SAYS THE ONE WITH THE CROW FOLLOWING HIM.

HMMMM. NOW I KNOW FOR CERTAIN THAT GIRLS NEED MAKEUP TO TALK. MUST BE A STRONG CHEMICAL IN THE FOUNDATION THAT MINGLES WITH THE PHEROMONES THAT ALLOW FOR SPEECH.
YOU BETTER STOP OR I'LL SIC MY GRANNY ON YOU!
BUS STOP #
11
PLEASE! NOT GRANNY! SHE MIGHT TAN MY HIDE!
JUST GET ON THE BUS, BUMBLING ELDER-IN-TRAINING!
WOULD THE FOLLOWING STUDENTS COME TO THE OFFICE...CODY NICHOLS, DAMON QUINN, MELISSA BROWN, MARCUS BROWN...

I WANTED TO LET YOU KNOW ABOUT SOME SCHOLARSHIPS AND ABOUT A TRIP TO HAIDA GWAII FOR INDIGENOUS STUDENTS.
I'M NOT INDIAN, MR. PERRY.
MR. BROWN, YOUR MOTHER CALLED THE OFFICE AND SELF-IDENTIFIED AS INDIGENOUS.
UM. I DON'T THINK SO...
MARCUS IS INDIGENOUS? DIDN'T SEE THAT COMING!

HELLO.
HI.
WHAT'S UP, DAMON QUINN?
YOU KNOW HOW YOU WERE TALKING ABOUT YOUR MOM DRINKING AND HOW SHE COULD NEVER STOP?
WELL, I THOUGHT MARNIE QUIT FOR GOOD...BUT SHE'S PASSED OUT ON THE COUCH.
YEAH, THAT HAPPENS...RELAPSE IS A PART OF RECOVERY.
WHAT DOES THAT MEAN?
ALCOHOLISM IS A DISEASE AND IT'S REALLY HARD TO QUIT...PEOPLE DO SLIP AND DRINK AGAIN, BUT IT'S A PART OF THE WHOLE PROCESS.

MY MOM TRIED TO GIVE UP DRINKING SO MANY TIMES. I USED TO GO WITH HER TO THOSE MEETINGS THAT ARE SUPPOSED TO HELP YOU QUIT.
DRINKING TOO MUCH...A DISEASE. I DID COVER HER WITH A BLANKET THOUGH.
EVERY TIME SHE'D QUIT, I ALWAYS HOPED THAT IT WOULD BE THE TIME SHE FINALLY MADE IT STICK...SHE NEVER DID.
I'M SORRY, JOURNEY.
ON THE OTHER HAND, I HAVE A VERY GOOD GIGI WHO IS LIKE MY MOM NOW. I MISS MY MOM BUT I KNOW I'LL MEET WITH HER AGAIN. MY GIGI SAYS SO.
DRINKING AGAIN IS CALLED A RELAPSE? AND IT'S NORMAL?
YEAH, IT'S A PART OF RECOVERY. TRY NOT TO BE MAD AT HER. SHE CAN'T HELP IT, AND SHAMING HER OR BEING MAD AT HER COULD PUSH HER FARTHER OUT.
GOT IT.
HEY, THERE'S A SWEAT LODGE CEREMONY COMING UP. DO YOU WANT TO GO? IT'S A CEREMONY FROM YOUR NECK OF THE WOODS.
I'LL GO IF YOU GO.
DEAL.

HOWDY, DAMON QUINN. ANY MORE VISIONS LATELY?
NO, NOT SINCE THE LAST TIME I WAS HERE. YOU WERE IN IT, ACTUALLY.
HMMM... INTERESTING.
DUDE, YOU FELL ASLEEP AND YOU WERE SNORING, TOO.
OKAY, LET'S TALK. SOMETHING'S BOTHERING YOU. WHAT IS IT?
MY MOM WAS DRINKING AGAIN.
UM...HMMM.
I DID TALK TO MY GIRL...FRIEND...MY FRIEND...AND SHE TOLD ME ABOUT RELAPSING.
I HEAR YOU--YOU CARE ABOUT HER, AND YOU WANT HER TO BE SOBER.
YEAH...

ONEISSIN

WHAT IS THIS? WHERE ARE WE?
THIS IS A RESIDENTIAL SCHOOL.
WHY ARE WE HERE? HOW COME THERE'S ONLY INDIGENOUS KIDS HERE?
NOT SO LONG AGO, INDIGENOUS KIDS WERE FORCED TO LEAVE THEIR HOMES AND FAMILIES AND ATTEND RESIDENTIAL SCHOOLS ALL OVER NORTH AMERICA...
...WHAT WE CALL TURTLE ISLAND.
I STILL DON'T UNDERSTAND.
THAT LITTLE GIRL IS KI-TÂNISKOTÂPÂN, YOUR GREAT-GREAT-GRANDMOTHER. GO SAY HI TO HER.
KEEP GOING, THEY CAN'T HURT YOU. IT'S A VISION.
IT FEELS SO...DARK.

HI.
H-H-HI. WE AREN'T SUPPOSED TO TALK.
WHAT'S YOUR NAME? ARE YOU COLD? YOU'RE SHIVERING.
MY NAME IS MARNIE. I AM C-C-COLD.
WHY DON'T YOU GO INSIDE?
WE AIN'T ALLOWED.
WHY?
JUST 'CAUSE. WE AIN'T ALLOWED. THEY'LL HIT US IF WE DON'T L-L-L-LISTEN.
THEY'LL HIT YOU?
I'M SO S-S-SCARED. I WANNA GO H-H-HOME.
WHAT ARE YOU SCARED OF?
THEY'LL PUT MY MOM AND DAD IN JAIL.

WHAT CAN I DO TO HELP?
TELL MOMMY. TELL HER TO PLEASE COME G-G-GET ME.
ONEISSIN
WHY DID YOU BRING ME HERE?!
TO SHOW YOU WHERE YOU COME FROM.
I NEVER WENT TO RESIDENTIAL SCHOOL.
I KNOW, BUT A LOT OF YOUR FAMILY AND ANCESTORS DID.
YOU AND YOUR MOM ARE INTERGENERATIONAL SURVIVORS.
WHAT DOES ALL THIS HAVE TO DO WITH ME?
EVERYTHING.
IT'S THE REASON WHY YOUR GRANDMOTHER DRANK, THE REASON WHY YOUR MOM DRINKS.
THIS TRAUMA FLOWS THROUGH THE BLOODLINES AND INTO YOU, DAMON.

THESE ARE STORIES YOUR FAMILY DOES NOT TELL. YOUR MOM NEEDS SUPPORT, LOVE, AND UNDERSTANDING.
WE ARE ALL SURVIVORS, DAMON. BUT THE HEALING BEGINS WITH YOU.
I SWEAR WE REALLY GO ON THESE TRIPS. WOW, HE SNORES LIKE A FREIGHT TRAIN.
Z-Z-Z-Z

DAMON, COME SIT. I HAVE SOMETHING FOR YOU.
I DIDN'T REALLY KNOW WHAT TO DO WITH THIS. BUT NI-KÂWIY SAID I WOULD KNOW WHEN THE TIME WAS RIGHT.
THIS DRUM HAS BEEN IN OUR FAMILY FOR SEVEN GENERATIONS.
YOU'VE HAD IT ALL THIS TIME? I DREAMT ABOUT THIS, MOM!
DO YOU KNOW HOW TO TREAT THE DRUM?
THUM
THUM
THUM
YES, MOM. I KNOW NEVER TO LAY IT ON ITS FACE AND THAT I HAVE TO RESPECT IT BECAUSE AN ANIMAL GAVE ITS LIFE...
HOW DO YOU KNOW ALL THESE THINGS, DAMON?

MOM, WAS YOUR GREAT-GRANDMOTHER IN RESIDENTIAL SCHOOL? WAS HER NAME MARNIE TOO?
HOW COULD YOU KNOW THAT?
HEY, THAT'S MY COFFEE.
NOW TELL ME HOW YOU KNOW ALL THOSE THINGS.
I'M LEARNING THINGS IN MY DREAMS. I EVEN MET MARNIE...OUR RELATIVE MARNIE.
SHE SAID SHE WANTED TO GO HOME AND THAT SHE WAS SCARED. HER MOM AND DAD WOULD HAVE BEEN THROWN IN JAIL IF THEY TRIED TO KEEP HER.
MOM, I'M SORRY FOR EVERYTHING THAT HAPPENED TO YOU AND OUR ANCESTORS.
I WANT YOU TO STAY SOBER...AND I'M LEARNING ABOUT RELAPSE...I'M NOT JUDGING YOU.

THAT BUILDING WAS BLACK LAST TIME!
COME IN!
YOU MUST BE HERE FOR THE INTERVIEW?
A GOOD FRIEND OF MINE RECOMMENDED YOU. SAID YOU'RE A DREAM TO WORK WITH, DAMON QUINN.
YOU'D BE CLEANING THIS BUILDING, 20 HOURS A WEEK. YOU CAN DO IT AFTER SCHOOL AND ON WEEKENDS. SOUND GOOD?
THAT WORKS, YES, THAT WORKS. UM, HAVE YOU ALWAYS BEEN IN THIS OFFICE?

I'VE BEEN IN THIS OFFICE FOR ABOUT TEN YEARS. NOW LET'S GET YOUR SCHEDULE FIGURED OUT.
SURE... SOUNDS GOOD.
FWOOSH

HEY, KIDDO.
MOM, THAT COUNSELLOR YOU FOUND? HOW DID YOU FIND HIM?
I MET THIS OLD INDIGENOUS GUY AT THE BUS STOP. I WAS CRYING AND I ENDED UP TELLING HIM EVERYTHING. HE GAVE ME CRAIG BEN BOLTON'S CARD.
CAN I SEE HIS CARD AGAIN?
SURE. IT WAS A COLOURFUL CARD. HANG ON. IT'S HERE SOMEWHERE.
HERE IT IS!

CBB Contract
Cleaning,
Worldwide
411 Cedar Road
IT'S A CLEANING BUSINESS CARD, MOM.
IS IT? I DIDN'T HAVE MY READING GLASSES ON...WRONG CARD...WAIT, LET ME LOOK SOME MORE.
CBB Contract
Cleaning,
Worldwide
411 Cedar Road
NO...IT'S OKAY, MOM. IT'S ALL GOOD.

CBB Contract
Cleaning,
Worldwide
411 Cedar Road

Time to Explore!

TO BE CONTINUED...

When I was growing up on the Kehewin Cree Nation, which is a reserve in Alberta, I read many books. I read the Little House on the Prairie series, the Nancy Drew series, and other books that told stories about family and home life. These stories showed a different world from the one I lived in—the world of my reserve, which experienced serious social problems like abuse, addiction, loss of parents and traditional parenting, and incarcerated family members. People like my family and me were never portrayed in such books.

While these books provided an escape from the world I was living in, they did not help me navigate my world. The stories I read made me feel like my life and experiences were mine alone—so I hid the secrets of my world from others. My reality was not that different from other Indigenous children, but there just weren't any stories out there that represented our lives or showed us ways to deal with our experiences that would keep us intact. This made me feel very alone. It was difficult for me to explain my experiences to others. My life would have been easier if I had been able to access books that I could see myself, my community, and my experiences in. Such stories would have given me a sense of hope and belonging.

Because I didn't see my own experiences reflected in books, I felt like I was somehow broken and that I had to hide my "brokenness" from everybody. If people knew what was really happening to me, they would think differently of me—and perhaps even hate me. I believed the narratives of Native savagery and unworthiness; at that time, they were the stories in history books and reflected what I had personally witnessed on the reserve.

Instead of creating space for me to think critically about Canada's history and its relationship with Indigenous Peoples, these stories perpetuated negative stereotypes about Indigenous people like me. They had a deep and lasting impact, not just on me, but across entire communities and family systems that identified as Indigenous. Because of these negative stories and stereotypes, many people felt it was a shameful thing to be Indigenous and some even denied their Indigenous heritage. Social problems like alcohol and drug addiction were portrayed as "Native problems" rather than the result of problems caused by colonialism, such as the breakdown of family systems and the loss of language, culture, and traditional parenting.

The realities of my childhood made me want to write books that Indigenous children and youth could see themselves and their experiences in. I want to show that Indigenous people can talk about their social problems and connect to our history in a way that allows critical thinking and growth. Alongside Damon, a young person making his way in today's world, I chose to include historical figures like Chief Big Bear in my story because he was known for helping his people through conflict during the North-West Rebellion. Chief Big Bear was a respected leader within his community and worked with other leaders like Chief Kehewin and Chief Sweetgrass to inform his people about the impacts of signing Treaty 6. Like Damon, readers can reflect on the strength and determination of their ancestors and bring those values into the future to continue making a positive impact in their communities.

Wanda John-Kehewin

WANDA JOHN-KEHEWIN (she, her, hers) is a Cree writer who uses her work to understand and respond to the near destruction of First Nations cultures, languages, and traditions. When she first arrived in Vancouver on a Greyhound bus, she was a pregnant nineteen-year-old carrying little more than a bag of chips, a bottle of pop, thirty dollars, and hope. After many years travelling (well, mostly stumbling) along her healing journey, Wanda brings her personal experiences to share with others. Now a published poet and fiction author, she writes to stand in her truth and to share that truth openly. Wanda is the mother of five children, one dog, two cats, and one angelfish, and grandmother to one super-cute granddog. She calls Coquitlam home until the summertime, when she treks to the Alberta prairies to visit family and learn more about Cree culture and tradition. *Visions of the Crow* (Dreams, Volume 1) is her debut graphic novel.

NICOLE MARIE BURTON (she, they) is a comics artist and children's book illustrator living on unceded Algonquin land. Born in the US and now based in Ontario, she is a founding member of the Ad Astra Comix publishing collective. nicole's work focuses on comics with social justice themes, including topics from Canadian history to the science of climate change. Her published works include *The Beast: Making a Living on a Dying Planet*, *The Boy Who Walked Backwards*, and a chapter in the anthology *Drawn to Change: Graphic Histories of Working Class Struggle*.

KIELAMEL "KIELA" SIBAL (she, her) is a Filipino Canadian letterer, graphic designer, cartoonist, writer, and illustrator. She is passionately curious about the craft of different storytelling methods, from comics and video games to film and illustration. Born in Pampanga, Philippines, Kiela currently conducts her sparkling antics of wizardry in Winnipeg, Manitoba.

A road trip back to Kehewin reserve is a chance for Damon to reconnect with his mom and family. But he has a secret—a secret that threatens to ruin everything.

DREAMS will return with

- new characters
- new visions
- and new adventures!

Scan the QR code to find out more.

Funded by the Government of Canada
Financé par le gouvernement du Canada | Canada

Canada Council for the Arts | Conseil des arts du Canada

HighWater Press gratefully acknowledges the financial support of the Government of Canada and Canada Council for the Arts as well as the Province of Manitoba through the Department of Sport, Culture and Heritage and the Manitoba Book Publishing Tax Credit for our publishing activities.

HighWater Press is an imprint of Portage & Main Press.
Printed and bound in Canada by Friesens
Design by Jennifer Lum
Cover Art by nicole marie burton
Lettering by Kielamel Sibal

Library and Archives Canada Cataloguing in Publication
Title: Visions of the crow / Wanda John-Kehewin ; nicole marie burton.
Names: John-Kehewin, Wanda, 1971- author. | burton, nicole marie, artist.
Description: Series statement: Dreams ; volume 1
Identifiers: Canadiana (print) 20230140882 | Canadiana (ebook) 20230140904
ISBN 9781774920459 (softcover) | ISBN 9781774920565 (EPUB) | ISBN 9781774920572 (PDF)
Subjects: LCGFT: Graphic novels.
Classification: LCC PN6733.J5 V57 2023 | DDC 741.5/971—dc23

26 25 24 23 1 2 3 4 5

MIX
Paper from responsible sources
FSC® C016245

HIGHWATER PRESS

www.highwaterpress.com
Winnipeg, Manitoba
Treaty 1 Territory and homeland of the Métis Nation